Franklin's Music Lessons

From an episode of the animated TV series *Franklin,*
produced by Nelvana Limited, Neurones France s.a.r.l. and
Neurones Luxembourg S.A., based on the Franklin books
by Paulette Bourgeois and Brenda Clark.

Story written by Sharon Jennings

Illustrated by Sean Jeffrey, Alice Sinkner and Shelley Southern.

Based on the TV episode *Franklin Takes a Music Lesson,*
written by Mark Mayerson.

Kids Can Read is a trademark of Kids Can Press Ltd.

Franklin

Franklin is a trademark of Kids Can Press Ltd.
The character Franklin was created by Paulette Bourgeois and Brenda Clark.
Text © 2002 Contextx Inc.
Illustrations © 2002 Brenda Clark Illustrator Inc.

Kids Can Press acknowledges the financial support of the Ontario Arts Council,
the Canada Council for the Arts and the Government of Canada, through the
BPIDP, for our publishing activity.

Kids Can Press Ltd.
2250 Military Road
Tonawanda, NY 14150

www.kidscanpress.com

Edited by Tara Walker
Designed by Stacie Bowes

Printed in Hong Kong, China, by Wing King Tong Company Limited

US 02 0 9 8 7 6 5 4 3 2 1
US PA 02 0 9 8 7 6 5 4 3 2 1

National Library of Canada Cataloguing in Publication Data

Jennings, Sharon
        Franklin's music lessons

US ed.

(Kids Can Read)
The character Franklin was created by Paulette Bourgeois and Brenda Clark.

ISBN 1-55337-171-2 (bound)   ISBN 1-55337-172-0 (pbk.)

I. Jeffrey, Sean II. Sinkner, Alice III. Southern, Shelley IV. Bourgeois, Paulette V.
Clark, Brenda VI. Title. VII. Series: Kids Can Read (Toronto, Ont.)

PS8569.E563F7195 2002a   jC813'.54   C2002-900265-6
PZ7J429877Frm 2002

Kids Can Press is a **ᐸᎾᴦᑌᔑ**™ Entertainment company

Franklin's Music Lessons

Kids Can Press

Franklin can tie his shoes.

Franklin can count by twos.

But Franklin cannot play the piano.

Franklin wants to play the piano.

He just doesn't want to practice.

This is a problem.

On Monday, Mr. Owl said,

"Today, we will not have math."

"Hooray!" said the class.

"Today, Mrs. Panda will teach us music."

Mrs. Panda sat at the piano.

She played "Row, Row, Row Your Boat."

Everyone clapped.

"This time," said Mrs. Panda,

"you will count one, two, three, four

over and over when I play."

"Is this math?" asked Franklin.

"No," said Mrs. Panda.

"This is how we count to the beat."

Mrs. Panda played.

The class counted.

Mrs. Panda opened
a big box.
She gave everyone
an instrument.

She gave out
instruments to toot
and instruments
to clang.

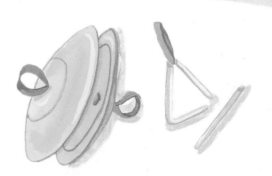

She gave out
instruments to bang
and instruments
to shake.

She gave Franklin
a bell to ring.

"Now everyone can play to the beat,"

said Mrs. Panda.

"One, two, three, four.

Who wants to show us how?"

Franklin put up his hand.

Ring, ring, ring, ring,

went Franklin.

Everyone clapped.

Mrs. Panda played

"Row, Row, Row Your Boat."

The class played their instruments.

Toot, toot,

toot, toot.

Clang, clang,

clang, clang.

Bang, bang,
bang, bang.

Shake, shake,
shake, shake.

Ring, ring,
ring, ring.

The music lesson was over.

"Good work," said Mrs. Panda.

"I will be back next week."

"Hooray!" said the class.

"Please keep your instruments,"

said Mrs. Panda,

"and play them every day.

Practice makes perfect."

Beaver gave her instrument

back to Mrs. Panda.

"I don't need it," said Beaver.

"*I'm* taking piano lessons.

Next week, I will play

'Row, Row, Row Your Boat'

on the piano."

"Very good, Beaver!" said Mrs. Panda.

"Hmmm," said Franklin.

Franklin ran home from school.

"I want to take piano lessons,"

he told his mother.

"Good for you," she said.

"Granny can teach you."

Franklin smiled.

"Piano lessons will be lots of fun!"

he said.

Franklin walked to Granny's house.

He met Beaver on the way.

"I just finished my piano lesson,"

said Beaver.

"You take lessons with my granny?"

asked Franklin.

"I've been taking lessons for ages,"

said Beaver.

"Today is my first lesson,"

said Franklin.

"I want to play

'Row, Row, Row Your Boat,' too."

"Remember," said Beaver,

"practice makes perfect."

Franklin sat at the piano.

Granny showed him

how to play a scale.

"Can I play 'Row, Row, Row Your Boat?'"

he asked.

"First you have to play the scale,"

said Granny.

Franklin played.

"Now again," Granny said.

Franklin played the scale

again and again.

"Very good," said Granny.

"Come back tomorrow."

Franklin went back the next day.

He played the same scale

again and again and again.

"Practice makes perfect,"

said Granny.

"Can I play

'Row, Row, Row Your Boat' now?"

Franklin asked.

"Not yet," said Granny.

Franklin frowned.

Piano lessons were not lots of fun,

he thought.

On Wednesday, Franklin had

a baseball practice.

On Thursday, he had a baseball game.

On Friday, he had

another baseball practice.

On Saturday, he had

another baseball game.

And on Sunday,

Franklin played baseball

with his friends just for fun.

Franklin did *not* play the piano

on Wednesday,

Thursday,

Friday, Saturday or Sunday.

On Monday, Mrs. Panda asked Beaver to play "Row, Row, Row Your Boat." "Maybe Franklin would like to go first," said Beaver.

"No," said Franklin.

"I cannot play

'Row, Row, Row Your Boat.'

I did not practice."

Beaver smiled.

"I practiced every

day this week,"

she said.

Beaver played the piano.

Everyone else played their instruments.

Toot, toot, toot, toot.

Clang, clang, clang, clang.

Bang, bang, bang, bang.

Shake, shake, shake, shake.

RING! RING! RING! RING!

Franklin's arm was so strong

from playing baseball ...

... that no one could hear anyone else.

"You are the best bell ringer

I ever heard,"

said Mrs. Panda.

"Thank you," said Franklin.

"Baseball practice makes perfect."